PEACEKEEPERS

Alan Trussell-Cullen

Australia • Brazil • Japan • Korea • Mexico • Singapore • Spain • United Kingdom • United States

Peacekeepers

Fast Forward
Level 13

Text: Alan Trussell-Cullen
Text: Alan Trussell-Cullen
Editor: Kate McGough
Designer: Vonda Pestana
Series Designer: James Lowe
Production Controller: Emma Hayes
Photo Research: Gillian Cardinal
Audio recordings: Juliet Hill, Picture Start
Speakers: Matthew King and Abbe Holmes
Reprint: Siew Han Ong

Acknowledgements
The author and publisher would like to acknowledge permission to reproduce material from the following sources: Photographs by AAP/AFP, cover, backcover, pp. 1, 9, 13 top/ Al Green, p. 4/ Gary Ramage, p. 5/ Karen Prinsloo, p. 8/ Sgt W. Guthrie, p. 15/ Behrouz Mehri, p. 16/ Jorden Baker, p. 18 left/ John Toohey, p. 18 right/ Yuri Cortez, p. 19 right; Australian Picture Library/Corbis/Jean Guichard, pp. 3, 21 bottom/ Howard Davies, p. 12/ Patrick Robert, p. 13 bottom/ Les Stone, p. 20/ Peter Turnley, pp. 22, 23; Getty Images/U.S. Navy, p. 11/ Paula Bronstein, pp. 17, 21 top/ AFP, p. 19 top; photolibrary.com/Imagesource, p. 6 top/ Digital Vision, p. 6 bottom; United Nations, pp. 10 (photo 203232), 14 (photo 203233).

ISBN 978 0 17 012579 6
ISBN 978 0 17 012573 4 (set)

Cengage Learning Australia
Level 5 , 80 Dorcas Street
Southbank VIC 3006
Phone: 1300 790 853
Email: aust.nelsonprimary@cengage.com

For learning solutions, visit cengage.com.au

Printed in China by 1010 Printing International Ltd
12 13 14 15 26

This product is made from materials that are compliant with the EU Deforestation Regulation

Evaluated in independent research by staff from the Department of Language, Literacy and Arts Education at the University of Melbourne.

PEACEKEEPERS

Alan Trussell-Cullen

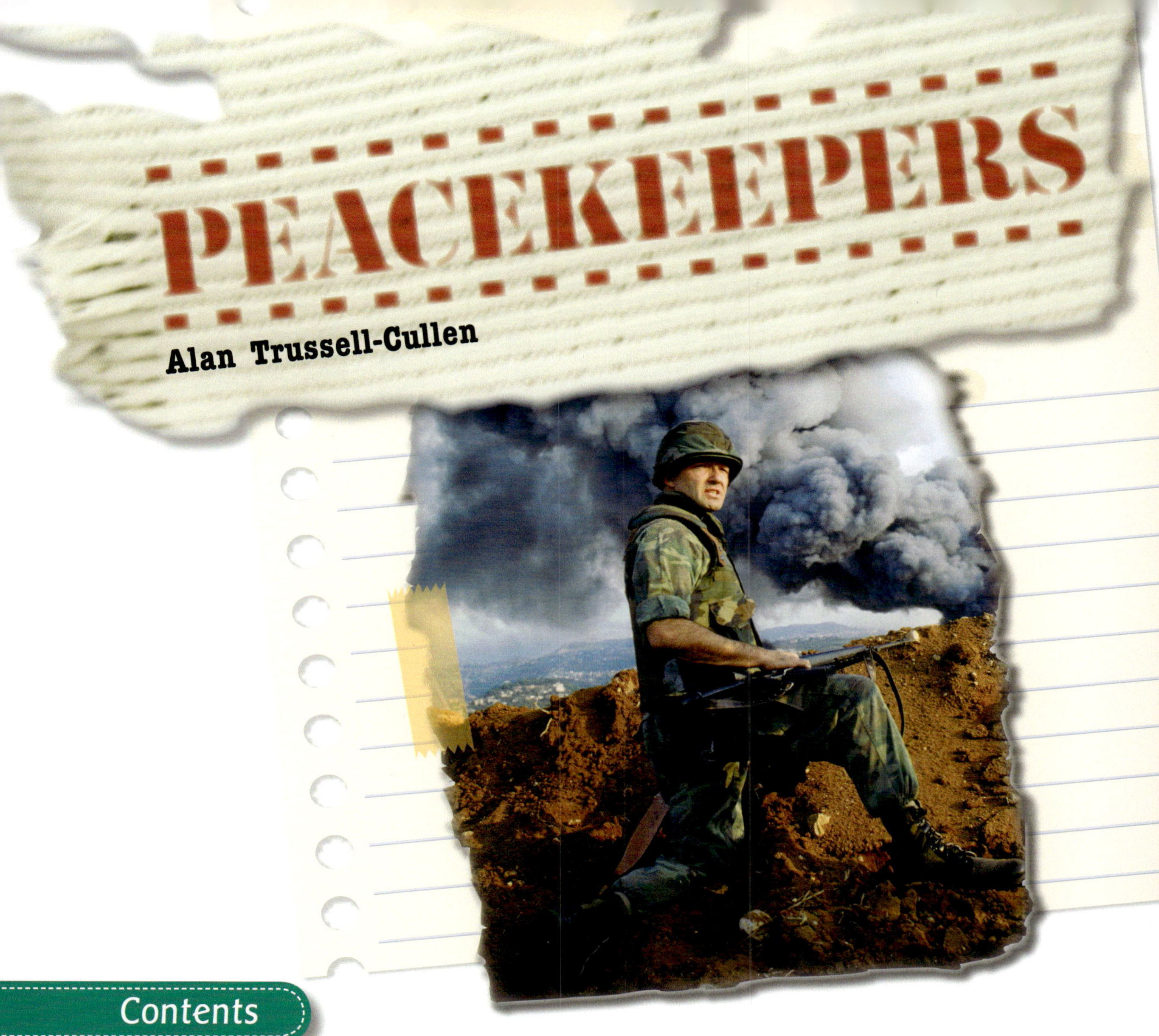

Contents

Chapter 1

PEACEKEEPERS

Peacekeepers are people who are sent to places where there has been fighting.
Peacekeepers help and protect people so they can feel safe, and so they can live together in peace.

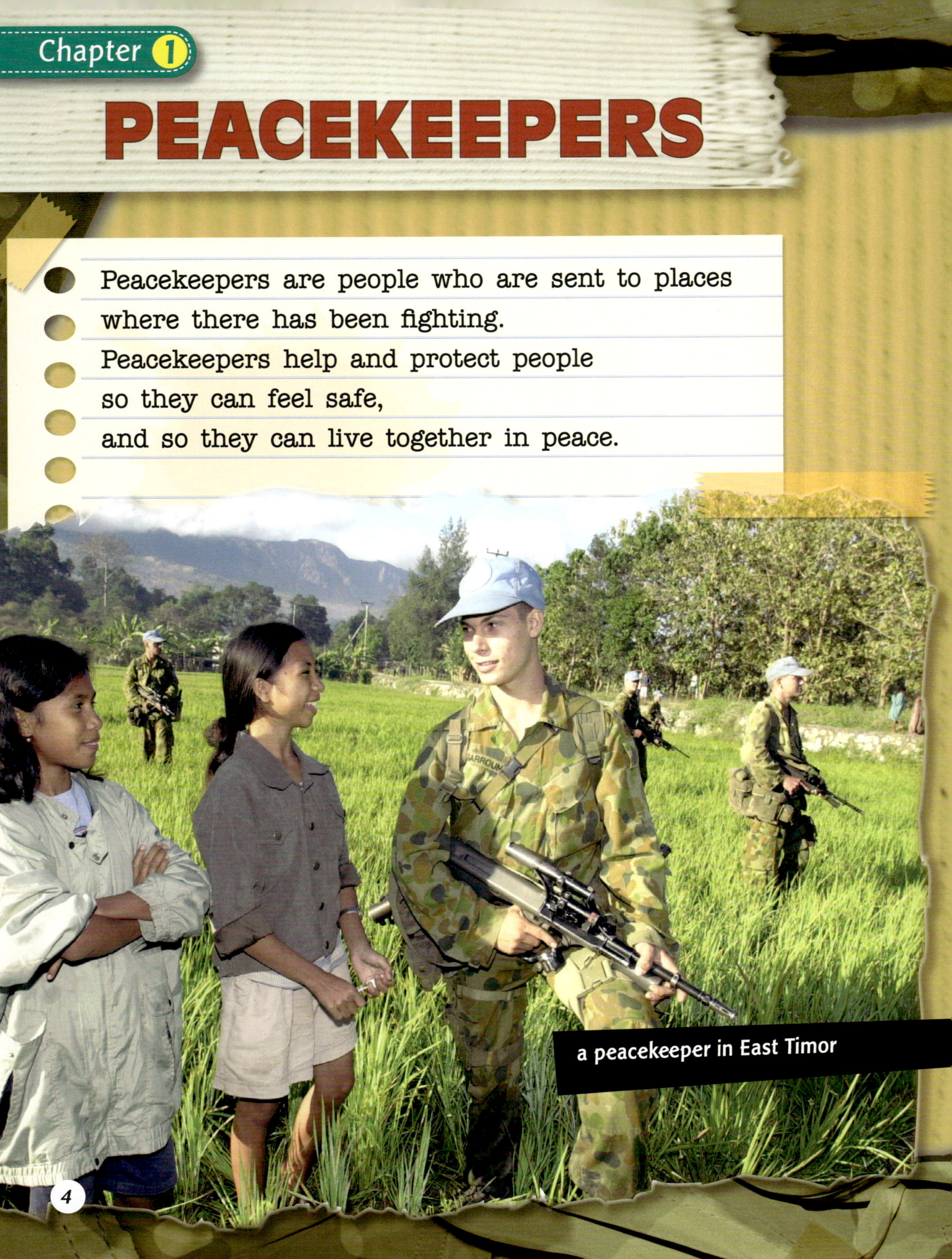

a peacekeeper in East Timor

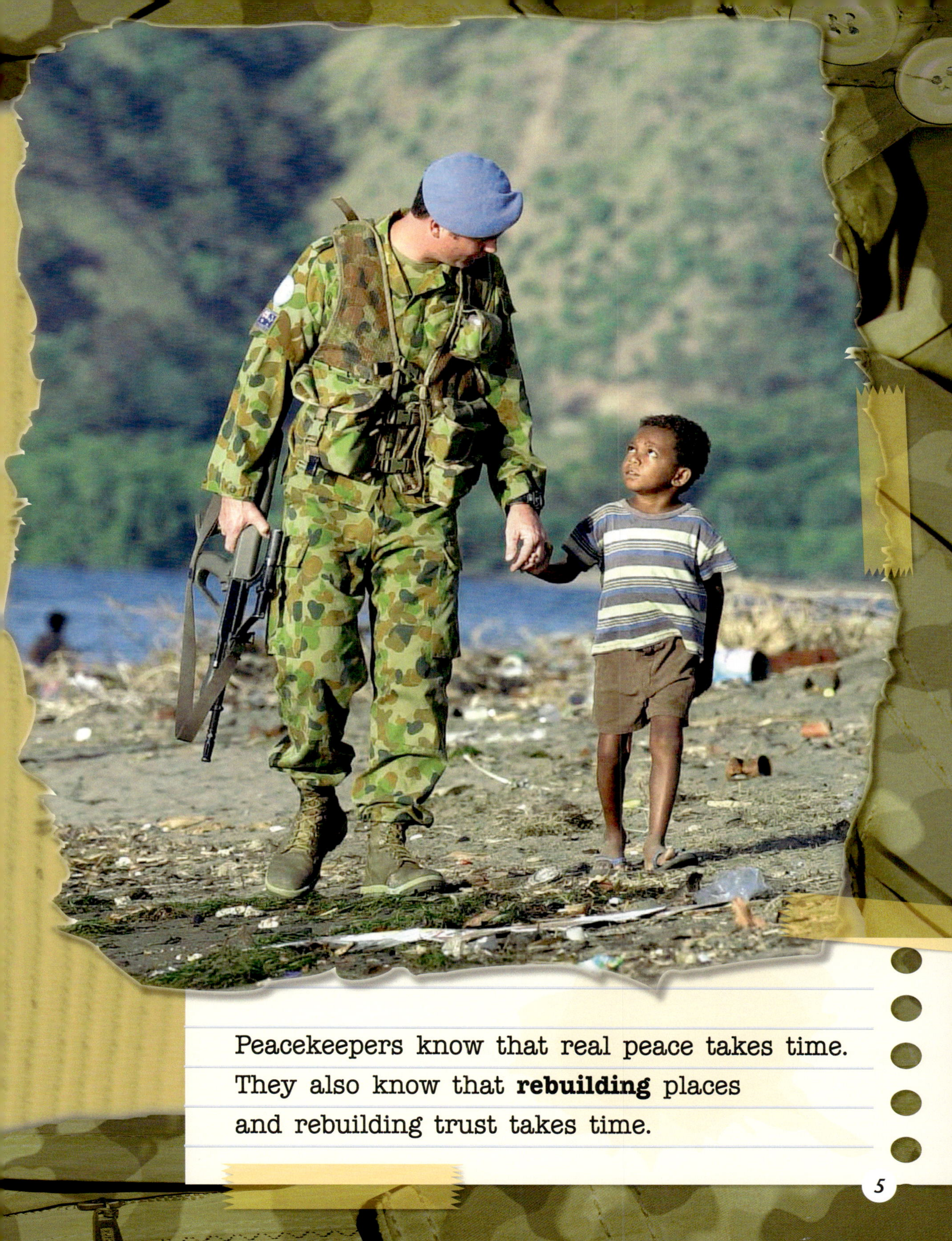

Peacekeepers know that real peace takes time. They also know that **rebuilding** places and rebuilding trust takes time.

THE UNITED NATIONS

Peacekeepers are sent to many different parts of the world by the United Nations.

The United Nations is an organisation that most countries in the world belong to.

United Nations

United Nations building in Geneva, Switzerland

Guatemala

Members of the United Nations meet together to help each other and to try to solve problems all over the world.

One way they try to solve problems is by sending groups of peacekeepers to countries where there is fighting or war.

The red dots on the map of the world show places where peacekeepers have been at work.

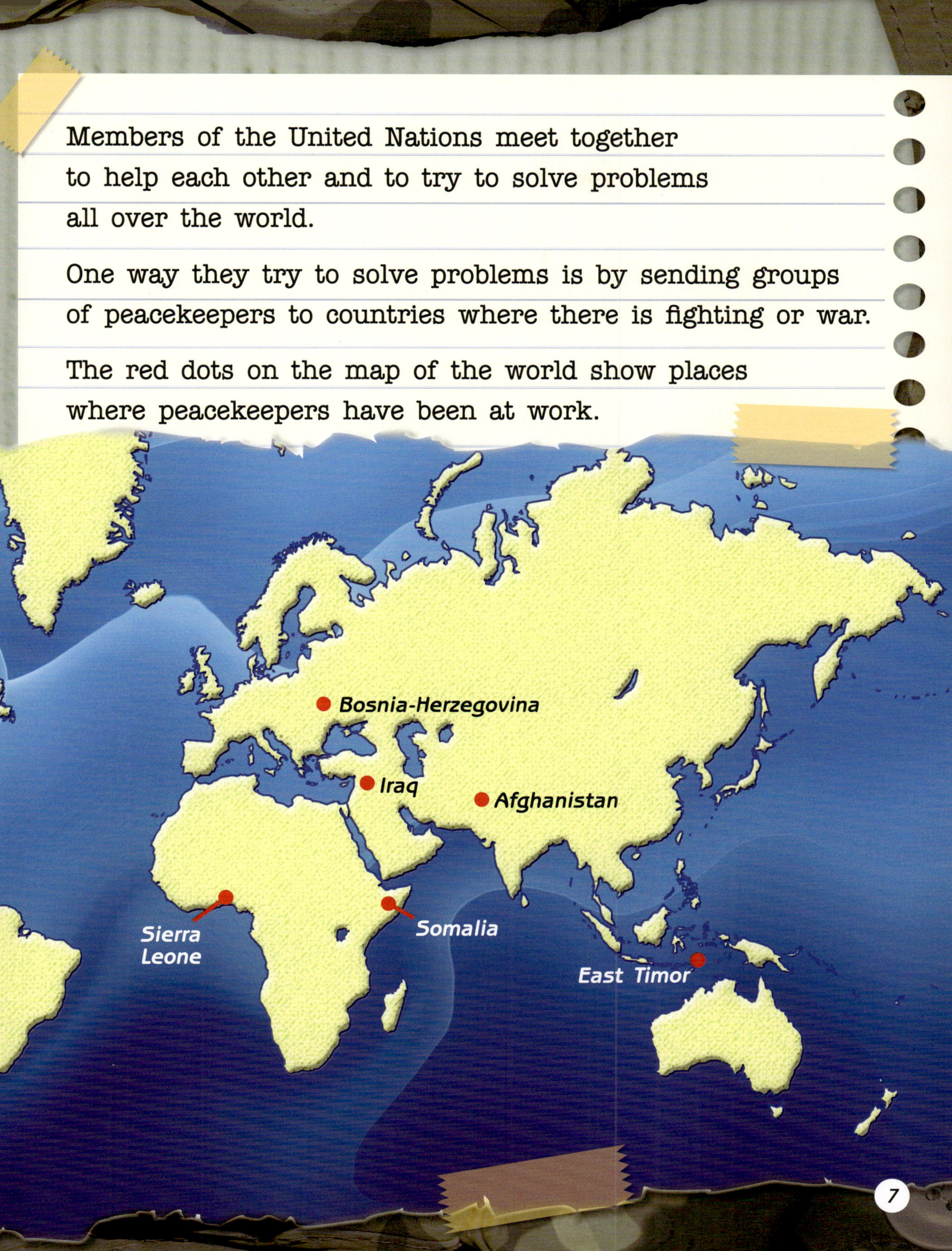

Chapter 3

WHAT PEACEKEEPERS DO

One of the first things peacekeepers do is to help people stay safe. That's why many peacekeepers are soldiers.

a soldier in Uganda, Africa

a soldier in Lebanon

If a country in need is unsafe,
peacekeeping and peace-building are very difficult.

Peacekeepers also help rebuild the country's roads and bridges so people can move about.

Peacekeepers help to give people clean water and take care of **refugees**.

Refugees are people who have had to leave their homes because of war.

Peacekeepers also build houses so people have somewhere to live.

Peacekeepers also take care of people's health.
Sometimes, they move people living in camps
to cleaner living places.
Some peacekeepers are doctors,
and others help doctors do their work.

This doctor can help look after people because peacekeepers have made the country safe.

Peacekeepers also take special care of children.
They build schools,
and sometimes they help teach the children.
Schooling is a very important part of rebuilding countries where there has been war.

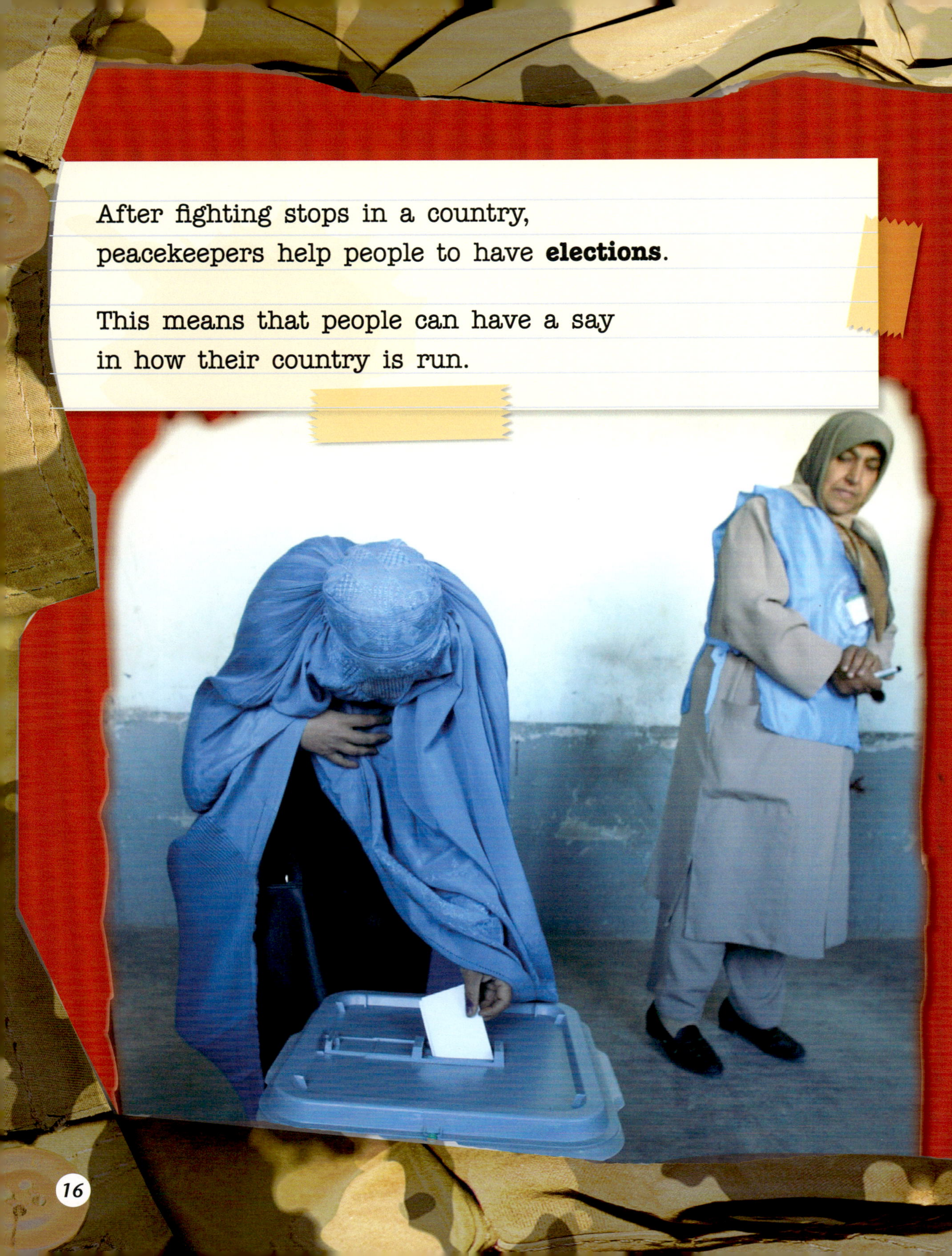

After fighting stops in a country, peacekeepers help people to have **elections**.

This means that people can have a say in how their country is run.

Peacekeepers help to run fair elections and teach people about voting.

Chapter 4

BEING A PEACEKEEPER

The life of a peacekeeper can be hard. Peacekeepers have to leave their homes and families and travel to other parts of the world.

Sometimes, they are only given a few days to get ready to leave.

Life can also be hard when peacekeepers arrive in a new country.
Sometimes, they have to face dangers.
They may not speak or understand the language of the people they are sent to help.

The weather and the food can be different
from what they are used to.
Sometimes, they live in tents.

Chapter 5

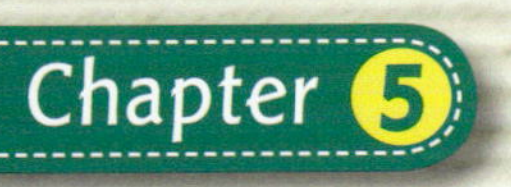

WHY PEOPLE BECOME PEACEKEEPERS

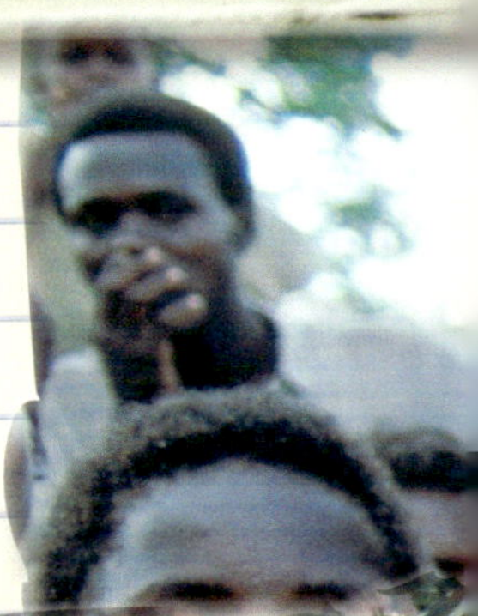

People become peacekeepers
because they want to help other people.
The best thanks they get are
the smiles and love of the people they help.

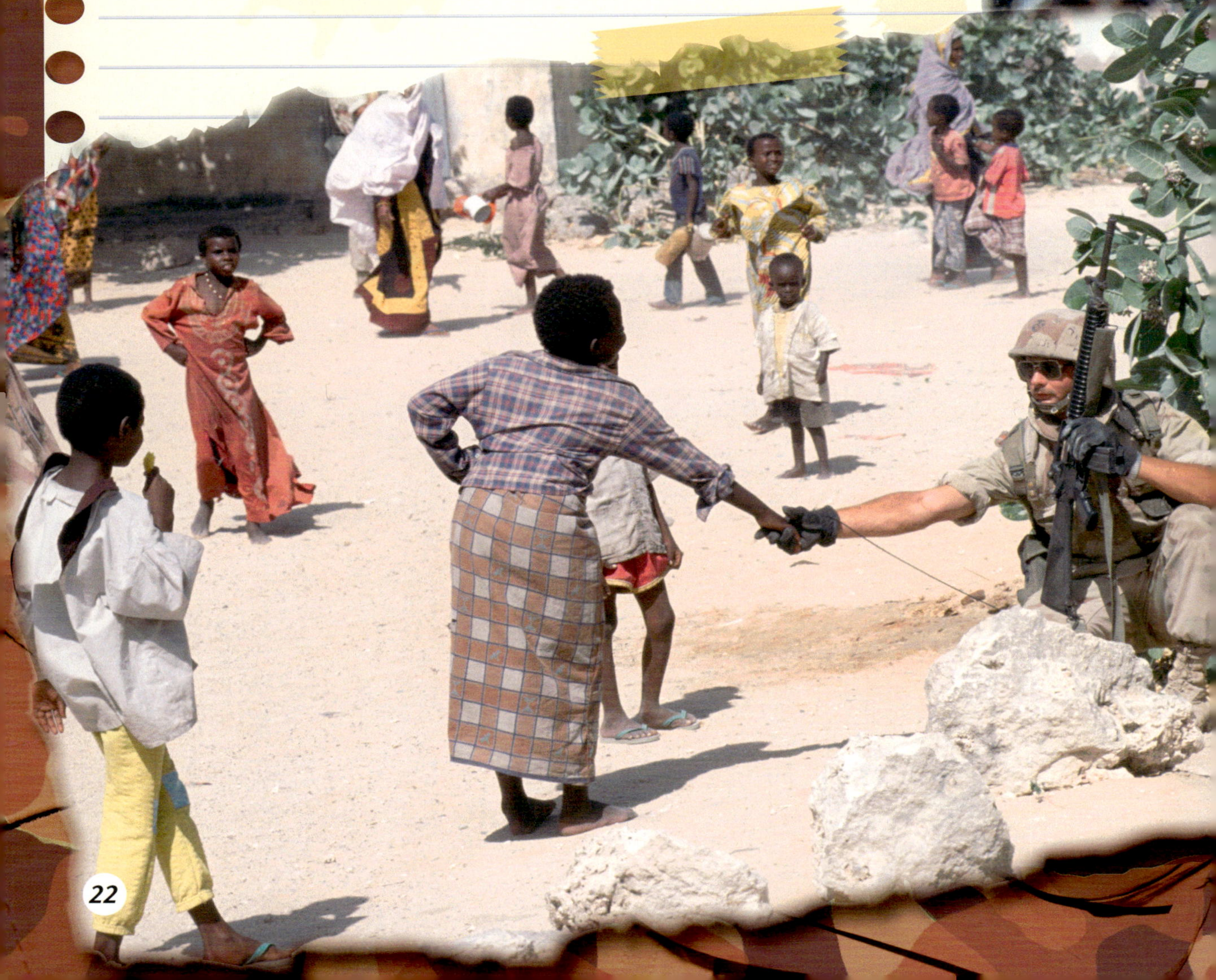

Glossary

elections when people choose their leaders by voting

rebuilding putting something back together, or making it better

refugees people who have had to leave their homes because of a war or other disaster

Index